JEERING BULLIES

"Hey, look at Petey," yelled Jasper MacMillan. "Petey's in a ring full of girls!"

Hump started hooting, "What's a boy doing in the *Maiden* class?"

Pete was so upset that he dug his right heel into the horse's ribs. All he could think of was getting away from the heckling voices. Casper took the bit in his teeth, and bolted. All Pete could do, in the crowded ring, was try to avoid running anyone over.

"Petey!" His mother shrieked in horror, seeing her son's horse out of control. Casper shied and bucked. Pete went flying.

At that moment, Peter realized that there was something worse than being THE ONLY BOY IN THE RING

THE DUTCH MILL STABLE STORIES

Kids who love horses: rich kids, poor kids, good kids, spoiled kids, girls, boys—you'll meet them all at the Dutch Mill Stables. Where young people have wonderful, heartwarming adventures and learn important lessons about riding, horse care, friendship, values—and, above all, about life.

A Dutch Mill Stable Story

THE ONLY BOY IN THE RING

NANCY WRIGHT GROSSMAN

Illustrated by
MARY DAMON

This is a work of fiction. All the characters and events portrayed in this book are fictitious, and any resemblance to real people or events is purely coincidental.

THE ONLY BOY IN THE RING

Cover art by Tim O'Brien

ISBN: 1-55902-984-6

First edition: January 1989

Printed in the United States of America

0 9 8 7 6 5 4 3 2 1

For Seamus
My One and Only Boy!

Chapter One

Lazy Daze
Comes to Stay

Pete Draper stuck his head out the window as his Uncle Will's big red and white horse van turned the corner and lumbered up the driveway toward Dutch Mill Stables.

"Hey, Tracy, I'm back! And wait'll you see what I brought with me!" Pete yelled to his friend, who was out sitting on the fence in front of the office.

Tracy jumped down and came running. The truck pulled up by one of the barn doors. The lettering on its side read, ELEVEN OAKS, ROYALTON, NORTH CAROLINA.

Pete hopped down from the cab and ran around to the side of the van. As soon as he and Uncle Will had opened up the doors and pulled out the ramp, Pete raced up it and into the huge nine-horse transport. Inside was one very lonely pony.

Pete threw his arms around Lazy. Lazy Daze had been Pete's to ride for the summer, and now he was Pete's for the rest of the year as well. He still couldn't believe it.

"Hey, Lazy!" Pete boomed. "You poor old thing, all by

yourself back here for all these miles. But it's okay now, we're here!" Lazy neighed in response to the good news.

Tracy came bounding up the ramp to see what all the fuss was about. "Wow, a pony!" she exclaimed. "Oh, she's cute! What did you call her?"

"Lazy. *His* name is Lazy Daze," Pete corrected her. "But I call him Lazy. Keith—he's my cousin—he calls him Crazy Daze because he used to drive Keith crazy. Keith has a horse now, so I got to ride Lazy this summer. Finally!"

Pete made a face. "I was getting real tired of Midget— you know, that little tiny pony I told you about, the one I outgrew ages ago. He was so short my feet would drag on the ground.

"Lazy and me, though, we get along great. I couldn't believe it when Uncle Will called up Mom and Dad and told them I could bring Lazy home with me if I wanted to—and they said yes!" Pete, barely able to contain his excitement, led the pony out of the van.

A few minutes later, Pete's parents rolled in and parked next to the truck. "Petey, Petey!" Mrs. Draper called to her son before the car had even stopped. Pete, like any normal ten-year-old boy, rolled his eyes.

"Hi, Mom. It's Pete, remember?" He dug the toe of his boot in the dirt. "Peter, if you have to. But, please, Mom, no more Petey, okay?"

"My, look how you've grown! Look, Bob, look how tall Petey's gotten!" was his mother's only response to his usual complaint. Then she exclaimed, "Oh, why look—is that your little brown horse?"

"Pony, Mom," Pete explained, patiently. "He's a pony. And he's not brown, he's a bay. He's a bay pony."

"Well, he certainly looks brown to me," Mrs. Draper insisted. "Looks awfully young, too."

"He's full grown, Mom. He's a full-grown pony. Good grief, he's fourteen years old. There's no way he's going to grow any more. And he's got a black mane and tail, so that makes him a bay. That's just the way it is, Mom," Pete tried to convince her. "Tell her, Uncle Will," he ended, lamely.

"Y'all listen to the lad, Eileen. He should know. He's been trained by the best—me!" Uncle Will said with a laugh.

"How are y'all?" he went on. "My, it's good to see you! Martha sends her love. She sure is gonna miss the boy." He put an arm around Pete. "Me, too, Pete," he added with obvious affection.

Pete had been spending his summers at Eleven Oaks in North Carolina with Uncle Will and Aunt Martha ever since he was five years old.

"It's a pretty weird sort of farm," Pete had tried to explain to one of his friends once. "The only things my Uncle Will raises are ponies and horses. He's always saying, 'Hmm, mighty fine crops of foals this spring' and 'Would you look at that crop of yearlings over there' like they were corn or carrots or something!"

The best thing about Pete's summers was learning how to ride well enough to keep up with his cousins, Keith and Kelly. Keith was four years older than he was. Kelly was a year younger than her brother, which made her three years older than her New Jersey cousin. All three had their own ponies to ride, and they spent many warm summer days playing cowboys and Indians, galloping through the undergrowth of Eleven Oaks's wooded pastureland.

Coming back home in September had always been hard for Pete, at least until this year. Last year he had discovered Dutch Mill Stables, the barn where several of his classmates kept their horses and took riding lessons. You didn't have to own your own horse to ride there. You didn't even have to be taking lessons to spend time at Dutch Mill, and Pete soon became a familiar sight around the barn, making himself useful wherever he could.

But this year everything was different. This year he was returning with a pony to ride! He would be able to take lessons with the other kids and maybe ride in shows. He'd go out riding on the trails, and, best of all, he would learn to jump. Uncle Will had been teaching Keith to jump this past summer. Now Pete would be able to learn, too.

Betsy Ingersol, the head trainer at Dutch Mill, came out to greet the new arrival. "Hi, Pete. Welcome back!" she called out warmly. "Looks like you're going to be one of our gang, now! We can always use another hand around here!"

She offered Lazy a hand to sniff and then ran her hand up the pony's face and scratched between his ears.

"So this is Lazy Daze, eh? You don't look so lazy to me," she commented with a chuckle. The pony's ears pricked up as he took in his new surroundings.

"No way! He's not lazy!" Pete stated firmly. "He's a lot of pony, right Uncle Will?"

"Nobody needs to speak for Lazy, lad. Or for y'all, I've noticed! Lazy'll make a name for himself 'round here, y'all see if he don't. Why, he'll be a reg'lar gentleman before ya bring him back next summer." He looked over at Pete. "Miz Ingersol tells me she's going to make a proper rider out of you, so's Keith and Kelly won't even recognize ya come next June!"

Pete smiled proudly. "You sure won't."

Chapter Two

Crawling Lessons

P ete became one of the most enthusiastic of Dutch Mill's many young riders. He was usually the first one there after school. He always ran all the way.

"It's a wonder you don't wear that pony's coat right off of him, laddie," old Mike, one of the grooms, had said more than once. Like everyone else around the barn, he marveled at the energy Pete put into the care of his pony. "There's nothing much I can be teachin' you on the subject of groomin' a horse, that's for sure!"

But there were many things Betsy could teach Pete on the subject of horsemanship. Pete had a *lot* to learn. She knew she had her work cut out for her from the first time she watched Pete ride.

"Young man, this is *not* a rodeo," Betsy called, laughing good-naturedly. "Come here and let me give you a few pointers."

Pete trotted over to where Betsy stood in the middle of the ring. "What's the matter?"

"Oh, just about everything, if you want to know the

truth! But don't let it bother you. How about we tackle one problem at a time, okay?" Pete nodded.

"Let's start with your legs. When you've got them where they belong and doing what they're supposed to be doing, we'll go on to the next thing."

Betsy came around, stood beside Lazy, and took Pete's leg and positioned it properly. "Okay, *this* is where your leg belongs," she showed Pete. "You've gotten used to riding with your legs too far in front of you, and that throws off the position of your upper body." She put a hand firmly in the middle of Pete's back and moved his upper body forward.

"Good. Now, let's see a little arch in your back. That's it, sit up really straight. Oh, does that ever look better!" she encouraged her new student.

"Okay, now that your leg knows where it should be, let's see you drop your heel. Heels down, toes up." Pete did as he was instructed.

"Can you feel that in your calf muscle?" Betsy asked.

Pete nodded. "I sure can. It feels weird."

"You'll get used to it. Okay, now, I want to see you stand up in your stirrups."

That's easy, Pete thought until he tried it. It took three tries before he got up and steadied. When he was finally standing, Betsy pointed out why it had been so hard.

"Look at your leg, Pete. See? It's where I showed you it should be. When you tried to get up, your leg went back to your old forward position and you fell backward, didn't you. Your leg has to be under you like this to give you a base of support. Can you feel it?"

Pete wasn't sure. "Move your leg forward like you used to and try to stand up," Betsy instructed. He couldn't. "Now, bring it back." Up he went with no trouble. A big grin spread across his face. "I learned something!"

"You bet!" Betsy smiled. "And you're going to learn lots more. Now, go out to the rail and walk."

"Walk?" Pete questioned.

"You have something against walking?" Betsy asked him.

"Well, no. I mean, I like to canter and gallop. I already know how to walk. Walking's boring," Pete complained.

"Walk!" Betsy commanded. She watched as he guided Lazy out to the rail. "Hey, Pete," she called to him, "do you remember how *you* learned to walk?"

A girl Pete didn't know trotted by him and giggled.

"No! I was a baby," Pete answered indignantly. This lesson felt pretty ridiculous all of a sudden.

"But you have a little sister, right? How old is Jenny?"

"She's five."

"Do you remember when she learned how to walk? How did she do it?" Betsy prompted him.

"She just got up and walked, I guess."

"After a lot of crawling and pulling herself up, and practicing holding on to somebody's hand or the furniture, right?"

"Yeah."

"Well, for the next few weeks, that's what you're going to be doing. Just think of it as crawling lessons. Don't be embarrassed. We all have to start somewhere!"

Chapter Three

Good Riding, Good Grades

"**I** think he's cute," Meg Walsh stated flatly. "Kind of young, but definitely cute." Meg was eleven.

"I think he's cute, too, and I don't think he's too young at all," ten-year-old Celia Mason said with a giggle. "Actually, Pete looks just exactly the right age."

Julia Jackson and Mel Hollister, who were both ten, nodded. They both liked Pete and always had. He had helped Mel on a lot of projects around the barn. Mel worked for Betsy to help pay the board bills for Streak, the pony she had leased from Julia's parents. Working for Betsy meant anything from pitching hay to painting jumps, and Pete was always ready to lend a hand.

Pete brought the number of boys who rode at Dutch Mill to a grand total of three. First there was Jonathan James Fitzpatrick III, who was thirteen and a serious show rider. Alexis Appleby, who turned twelve that year, considered Jonathan to be her own private property. As yet, however, she hadn't succeeded in making Jonathan aware of her feelings. He seemed to be more interested in Tracy Field. Bobby Williams, the only other boy, was seven.

Pete was surprised to find out how popular he had suddenly become. Being one of the three Dutch Mill boys was practically a full-time job.

"Want to come with us out on the trails?" offered Meg's twin sister Morgan. "We're going over to Murdock's Pond and back. And Julia and Mel are coming, too." She thought for a moment, then added, "We've got candy bars."

"I can't," Pete answered with a groan. "I've got a lesson with Betsy in fifteen minutes. Some other time, okay?"

He continued on down the aisle toward Lazy's stall. "Hey, Pete!" came a voice from behind him. He looked back to see Loretta leading her horse, Crazy Eddie, down the corridor. "Hiya, Loretta." Pete responded.

"Hey, Jody and I are going out for a ride on the Country Club trail. Want to come?" Loretta asked.

"Sorry, can't." Pete told her about his lesson.

"Well, we could wait till you're finished. It still stays light till about seven, so there's no big rush, right?"

"Gee, I'd like to, but I have to be home early tonight. It's my older sister's birthday."

Before he reached the ring, Pete had been invited on two more trail rides and on a ride and picnic for Saturday. That invitation he accepted.

Most afternoons, however, Pete spent his free time working—hard. He was determined to win Betsy's praise.

Betsy had lots of different ways of working with the kids she taught. With some she went slowly, concerned that they might quit if she pushed them too hard. With others, she bullied them a little bit, sensing that they responded well to being challenged. Pete was definitely the type who did his best when he was pushed.

"I'd say that was good—if I didn't know you could do better," Betsy told him after he'd executed a figure eight for her. His next one was faultless. "Yes! Yes! *That's* good riding!" She rewarded him with an approving smile.

Pete grinned ear to ear, collapsed on Lazy's neck and patted the pony vigorously. He never forgot that Lazy put in one-half of every good performance.

Pete's parents were concerned about another kind of

performance—Pete's school performance. His grades in school had never been great, and his mother feared that having the added distraction of the pony would make it just that much harder for Pete to concentrate on his schoolwork.

Lazy, in fact, had just the opposite effect on Pete.

"Petey, would you come in here please," Mrs. Draper called grimly to him one evening in November. Pete appeared at the door quickly, wondering what had prompted her serious tone of voice.

"Can you explain this to me, young man?" she asked, pushing a computer printout toward him. He looked at it with alarm.

"It's my midterm grades, isn't it?" he said, nervously.

"Yes, and they're excellent. What exactly is going on here?" She looked at him sternly and then started to smile, unable to keep up the pretense any longer. "I've got to admit, if anything Lazy seems to be having a good effect on your schoolwork. I'm really proud of you, and so's your Dad."

Pete let out a sigh of relief and decided to ignore this one "Petey."

Chapter Four

"It's Not Who Wins . . ."

Pete's days with Lazy flew by. The warm September afternoons had become crisp November afternoons, and evening came earlier and earlier. Before Pete knew it, it was Christmas.

"A show coat!" Pete let out a whoop, as he opened the biggest present under the tree first. Ever since he'd brought Lazy home with him, he'd been thinking about the day when he'd be ready to join all the other Dutch Mill kids who took their horses or ponies to the shows.

"Betsy gave us a few hints!" Mrs. Draper said as she hugged him. Pete jumped up to try on the navy blue coat, and Sarah, his older sister, surprised everyone when she admitted that she thought he looked sharp.

Santa also brought Pete a new pair of breeches, a pair of gloves, and a hunt cap. Pete was especially glad about the hat. His old one was looking pretty worn.

"All I have to do is give my boots a good polishing, and I'll be ready!" Pete crowed. He couldn't wait. He was over at the barn the next morning at eight o'clock, looking for Betsy.

"Hey, Betsy," Pete yelled when he finally saw her. "When's the next show? I got a coat for Christmas and I'm ready to roll!" He ran breathlessly up to her.

"Whoa there, pal!" Betsy answered laughing. "It's not quite that simple. It takes more than clothes to be ready for a show!"

"You mean I'm not ready yet? After all those lessons? Just two days ago you said I was doing great. Now I'm not?"

"You are. It's almost 'all systems go.' It's just that a few things still need some polishing up. Not your boots—they look terrific!"

Pete hardly heard the compliment. He tried to look indifferent, but he couldn't hide his disappointment.

"Oh, come on now, Pete. I'm not talking about years. A few more weeks. Anyway, the next show is the Green Tree, and that's a big one. That's no place for your first show." Pete still looked dubious. "Trust me," Betsy added.

The next several weeks taught Pete a lot about patience. He also worked harder than ever. Betsy drilled him mercilessly on lesson days, and instead of going out on the trails, he used his other afternoons to drill himself. One day in mid-February Betsy called him into the office.

"Now?" he asked expectantly.

"Now." Betsy nodded and grinned. "You're good and ready. You're *more* than ready, which is what you've got to be. You've really proven to me that you want to show and that you know your stuff."

Betsy handed him a prize list that described all the classes. Four Springs Farms was having a local show in three weeks. Pete's entries would have to be in by this Friday. He and Betsy talked about the classes he would try.

"I'm going to be honest with you, Pete," she told him seriously. "Lazy is a cute pony, but even braided up, he's not much to look at. He's what he is—a cute, fat pony.

"The fact is, you're going to have to work darned hard to even get noticed in the show ring. This may be just a local show, but I've got to tell you, kiddo, a lot of kids around here have some really flashy horses. I don't want you to be disappointed if you get overlooked, okay?"

Pete was sure that wouldn't bother him at all. "I just want to show. I don't care if I don't win," he insisted.

Betsy complimented him on his good attitude and started her usual pep talk about sportsmanship.

"I know, I know," Pete interrupted her. " 'It's not who wins . . .' My dad says it all the time."

Pete found himself repeating his father's words all that spring. "It's not who wins," he muttered to himself as he lined up in front of the judge in class after class, show after show, and each time he heard six other riders called out to receive their ribbons. By the time Uncle Will's van pulled into Dutch Mill that June, Pete had seven shows under his belt—and not a single ribbon on his wall.

Chapter Five

Green Horses
and Old Ponies

"Y ou're back!" Kelly yelled as the Eleven Oaks van pulled up the driveway. "Hey, Ma, Pete's back! Lazy's home!" Kelly ran across the gravel to meet her father, who stopped to let her step up on the running board and give him a welcome-home kiss. She rode up to the barn hanging tightly onto the door frame, bubbling over with questions.

"How's Lazy?" she shouted to Pete across her father. "Did everyone like him? Was he good? Did he miss us?"

"Everyone liked him fine, except the judges at the shows," Pete grumbled. "None of them even noticed him, not in a ring full of horses."

"But did he do good? Were ya good?" Kelly wanted to know.

"Yeah, we were great. Only it's the best kept secret in the entire state of New Jersey."

Pete and Kelly got Lazy out of the van, walked him around for a while to get the stiffness out of his legs, and then put him in his old stall. Lazy sniffed at the feed tub, the water bucket, and in the corners and then settled down.

15

Pete threw a handful of hay in for him, and pretty soon Lazy was chomping away contentedly.

Keith showed up as Pete and Kelly finished putting away Lazy's saddle and bridle. He had just finished riding and was still in his boots and breeches.

"Hey, Pete, how's it goin'," he drawled, sticking out a hand. Pete couldn't help thinking how tall Keith had gotten since last summer.

Keith seemed to read his thoughts. "Grew four inches. I'm fifteen, after all. I've jes' 'bout outgrown Ghost." Keith laughed. His voice was a lot lower now, too.

"Ghost?" Pete asked, confused.

"Ghost Story. The horse I've been ridin' this year. Him," he said, pointing down the aisle to a beautiful gray whose head was out its stall door. "That's Ghost."

Pete walked down and greeted Keith's horse. Keith came up behind him.

"He's okay. I've been showin' him since January. Took reserve junior hunter champion at Tryon. He was jumpin' real good there. He's not real consistent though. Jumps good some days, not so good other times. But Pa's watchin' out for a jumper for me. Somethin' a whole heck of a lot bigger. I want to show jumpers. Nobody cares what you look like—you jes' have to get over them fences."

Pete had seen a few junior jumper classes at the shows he'd entered back home. The Dutch Mill kids didn't ride in many of them. The jumps were big, and Betsy didn't want anyone picking up bad habits riding jumpers. Just as Keith had said, proper horsemanship didn't matter—all that counted was making sure your horse cleared the jumps.

"Hey, Pete, maybe Pa'll let y'all take Ghost home with you the end of the summer," Keith said slowly. "Yeah, if we find me a horse soon, maybe ya can get started riding Ghost before you go."

Pete's eyes got big and he found himself looking at the gray with much more interest. "How old is he?" Pete asked.

"Six. He was pretty green when Pa got him."

"He looks better gray," Pete joked.

Keith laughed, grabbing Pete and wrestling him into a

hammerlock in a matter of seconds. "Okay, okay," Pete gasped. "You win! He was green." It was the oldest joke in the horse book—a young, inexperienced horse was always referred to as 'green.'

"Think *you* could ride a green one?" Keith challenged his young cousin. "Lazy's no spring chicken. He's no big deal."

"You're telling me," Pete agreed glumly. "I've been showing him since the spring and nothing."

"Nothin'?" Keith was surprised.

"Nope," Pete admitted. "He didn't stand a chance in the middle of a bunch of classy horses."

"Didn't you show him in any pony classes? He always did okay in the pony division 'round here."

"Oh sure, pony classes too. Nothing."

The two cousins had wandered back over to Lazy's stall and were looking in on him. "He's showin' his age, that's for sure," Keith commented. "And he's gettin' fat. I guess his show days are 'bout over. It's lazy days ahead for ol' Lazy Daze."

Chapter Six

A Good Idea

I t didn't take Pete any time at all to get settled back in at Eleven Oaks. After one of Aunt Martha's great lunches, he galloped upstairs to unpack. Afterward he threw his jacket on the extra bed in Keith's room—which would be his for yet another summer—pulled on his boots, and ran back down to the barn.

Kelly and Keith were both in the tack room. Kelly was working away at a bridle that hung on the cleaning hook, and Keith was just getting down a saddle that needed attention. He swung it onto the saddle-cleaning stand and started soaping up a big sponge.

"So, you and Lazy didn't exactly take New Jersey by storm, eh, twerp," Keith kidded Pete. Pete grabbed another sponge from under the cleaning stand and let it fly at his cousin.

"Hey, buddy, you're playin' with dynamite now!" Keith grinned, dunking his sponge back in the bucket that stood beside him. He held up the dripping mass and started advancing toward Pete.

"No!" Kelly shrieked from behind him.

"Oh, so you're standin' up for the little guy, eh?" Keith called, not taking his eyes off Pete. "Y'all on the same team? It's the midgets 'gainst the men, is it?" Suddenly another wet sponge caught him on the back of the neck. Keith spun around, confronting Kelly in mock rage.

"So the pipsqueak wants to get into it. Okay, get into it!" His sponge flew.

Kelly ducked and the sponge sailed out the tack room door, landing squarely at Uncle Will's feet. He picked it up and raised his eyebrows questioningly.

"Uh-oh." Keith, Kelly, and Pete gulped in unison.

"Hmmm." Stepping into the tack room, Uncle Will barked, "If I didn't know better, I'd say that maybe a little less than a whole lotta work's gettin' done here today.

"Pete, whadaya say we take us a little walk and leave these younguns to their chores. Then when they're finished, you kids can go on down to the swimmin' hole and cool off." Uncle Will's broad wink made it clear that he wasn't half as angry as he had sounded.

Pete and his uncle wandered out of the barn and across the courtyard in front of it. Eleven Oaks's main barn was a beautiful brick structure shaped like three sides of a huge square. There were big planters trailing with red-flowered vines by all the doors and a pair of cast-iron jockey hitching posts stood guard by the main entrance. Their jackets were painted white with red sleeves, and their caps were red as well.

"Remember the first summer I came down here, Uncle Will?" Pete reminisced. "I wasn't any taller than those two jockeys!"

"You sure are taller now, lad," Uncle Will said with a twinkle in his eye. "Taller, and a lot smarter. You always was a smart one, though. You picked up everythin' there was to know about horses like you was born to it, boy.

"And your Miz Ingersol, she was tellin' me y'all're ridin' like a pro these days. She was tellin' me how hard it was for you at first, and how ya stuck with it and worked like a demon. Yep, that's what she told me," Uncle Will answered Pete's surprised stare.

"She said that?" Pete marveled. Betsy's compliments were so hard to come by that it even felt great getting one secondhand like this.

"That she did. And she also told me how frustrated you were gettin', what with tryin' to show that tired old pony we saddled you with. Don't worry—y'all don't have to be polite with your Uncle Will now. I know Lazy's fun for knockin' around the woods, but I also know he's no show pony anymore. But from what Miz Ingersol told me, you learned a whole lot on that little guy. I'm lookin' forward to seein' what kind of a rider y'all're becomin'!"

Pete took a deep breath. "Uncle Will, Keith said you're looking for a jumper for him and that he's outgrowing that gray horse, Ghost Story. He said maybe I could ride Ghost this summer . . ." Pete's nerve failed him and his voice trailed away. He gulped nervously.

Uncle Will looked the boy up and down. "Hmmm . . . Y'all are gettin' some size on you," he mused, half to himself. "And you're long 'nough in the leg. Hmmm . . ."

Uncle Will took his cap off and ran his hand through his hair. He always did that when he was deep in thought. Pete stood his ground and looked Uncle Will square in the eye.

"Yep," he nodded suddenly to the boy. "Good idea."

Chapter Seven

Send Betsy Back to Jersey

Pete held his nose as he jumped off the boulder and into the "swimmin' hole." An old rock quarry—the hole, as they'd come to call it—had served for many years as country club, secret headquarters, and proving ground for all the local kids. Boys and girls for miles around would long remember those first death-defying leaps into the hole's chilly waters.

Pete came bursting to the surface, whooping from the sudden cold.

"Whatsa matter, twerp," Keith taunted him from high up on the opposite wall. "Water not quite warm 'nuf for y'all? Shall I have the maid draw ya a hot bath?"

"Come on, chicken. Here, little chicky. Come on and jump off the little ledge and into the warm water, little chicky," Pete jeered in return. "Bok bok-bok-bok-bok!"

Keith launched himself into space, pulled his legs up and blasted the far reaches of the quarry with water as he landed in a perfect cannonball not a foot and a half from his nervy little cousin. He surfaced quickly, reached out, and pushed Pete under. Pete came up ready to take him on.

22

"Why, young man, don't you have any idea how dangerous that kind of behavior can be?" Keith acknowledged the danger by pushing Pete back under.

"Oh, please, kind sir, please, please don't do that to me again," Pete pleaded, grinning gamely as he came up again.

"I'm going to tell your mother on you," he said the third time.

The fourth time, Pete shot himself up into the air and came down with arms out and hands flat, sending a spray of water splashing in Keith's face. Then he struck out fast for the shore. He was lying back sunning himself on a rock and talking to Kelly when Keith came out of the water a few minutes later.

"So, Pa tells us ya went and learned how to be some fancy-pants rider," Keith started in again as he found himself a comfortable spot to sit. "Have ya gotten too big for yer fancy breeches, or are ya gonna keep on talkin' to us home-grown equestrians?"

"Oh, I'll probably keep talking to you," Pete said condescendingly, "if you try not to embarrass me too much. And if you're real polite, maybe I might even give you a pointer or two."

That was too much for Keith. He jumped to his feet, strode over to Pete, picked him up, and carried him to the water's edge. Pete nonchalantly crossed one leg over the other and acted as if being dumped back in the water was what he wanted to do more than anything else in the world. When he came sputtering to the surface, he said very politely, "Thank you, young man."

"You know, sometimes your legs are too far forward when you jump," Pete told Keith the next morning. "That's why you sometimes fall back over the fences, which is probably why Ghost doesn't jump real consistently. He's waiting to see what's going to happen over the next fence."

Keith glowered at his cousin. Pete was really beginning to get on his nerves. However, he did try adjusting his leg position to match Pete's. "That's it," Pete said.

Pete urged Lazy into a canter and stood up in his stirrups

in jumping position. "See, you need to keep your legs like this all the time. It helps keep you forward. Try it."

Ghost followed Keith's cues into a smooth canter and Keith attempted to mimic Pete's position. He found it very hard to maintain his balance for more than six or eight strides at a time.

"I don't see where's all this standin' up and bobbin' around's gonna make much difference over a jump course," Keith drawled.

"Betsy won't let you even try jumping till you can do this for hours without falling back. She makes you go around like this for weeks—for years! You feel real stupid, but she says it's important."

"Yeah? Well if Miz Betsy said it, it sure as shoot must be true," Keith said sarcastically. He'd already heard as much about Betsy as he could take. The way his father had been going on about Pete's lessons and Pete's trainer had really gotten to the older boy.

"You don't believe me? Hey, that's no skin off my nose," Pete said. He had heard his father use that expression many times. To his surprise, it seemed to work on Keith just as well as it had ever worked on him. It shut Keith up, anyway.

Pete continued to canter around, still standing in his stirrups. Finally Keith called out, "You sure can do that for ever, can't you." Then he tried it again.

After falling back several more times, Keith was about to give up in disgust. Pete rode up to him.

"Hey, don't quit. Try this. Grab a handful of Ghost's mane and use that for balance." Keith tried it and found it worked. Pretty soon the two cousins were challenging each other with circles and figure eights, all done standing in their stirrups. They looked like jockeys breezing their young colts as they galloped down the sides of the ring.

Keith tried jumping a few little crossbars. To his amazement, he felt steadier. Ghost seemed steadier, too. Pete sent Lazy over the same jumps and then pulled him up. Lazy and Ghost were heaving and sweaty from all the work, in spite of the early morning chill.

"How did that feel?" Pete asked.

"Not bad."

"It looked good. It looked smooth and steady and balanced, like—"

"Like Miz Betsy says, right? Look here, midget, I've gotta tell you, I sorta feel like this Betsy person's invaded this place, you know what I mean? Thing's was goin' along jes' fine till this Betsy showed up with you yesterday. How's about we send ol' Betsy on back up to Jersey, if it's all right with you, okay?"

Chapter Eight

Private Lessons

"**W**hat else am I doin' wrong?" Kelly wanted to know. Keith hated having Pete point out his faults, but Kelly didn't mind at all. She looked on Pete as her own private trainer.

"Your feet are sticking out too far," Pete yelled to her. "Turn them so they're pointing forward. Yeah!" Kelly was standing in her stirrups just like Pete had showed her.

"Now get your elbows in, too. And your shoulders back."

Kelly circled the ring twice at a trot and once at a canter. Then she popped Max over a two-foot post-and-rail jump. The pinto pony hardly broke stride. Kelly patted Max on the neck as she slowed him to a walk.

"You sure have picked up on how to teach folks," she observed as she and Max pulled alongside of Pete and Lazy. "You don't look like you used to, neither. Ya make me feel like a know-nothin'.

"I never really cared much before. But with Keith goin' to shows, and y'all ridin' like some kinda professional . . .

well, it makes me want to learn. Pa never taught us much—he jes' put us on the ponies and gave 'em a slap on the rear!" She gave Max an affectionate pat.

"I sure enjoy ridin'. I can't imagine not havin' a pony or a horse in my life. But now I think I'd like to be better at it. Would you teach me?"

"I'll teach you everything I know—which you'll see really isn't all that much," Pete admitted freely. "You're getting a real amateur, I'm warning you!"

"Will you give me real lessons, like every day?"

"Uh, well, sure. How about nine o'clock, Monday to Friday? Rain or shine."

"Rain or shine. Now what about Saturday and Sunday?"

"Hey!" Pete complained. "When are we supposed to have fun? Remember, this *is* summer vacation!"

The next morning, Pete was standing in the middle of the ring trying to look as official and professional as he could manage. It wasn't easy. His pupil was the same cousin he had clowned around with for six summers in a row, and at this moment she was sticking her tongue out at him.

"I said get your heels down further!" he hollered at the impudent Kelly.

"And I said they don't go no further," Kelly shot back, giggling.

"Okay, okay. But keep them down as far as you can. Now, instead of kicking Max, I want to see you squeeze him into a trot. No, I mean, I *don't* want to *see* you squeeze him into a trot. I shouldn't be able to see anything. At the moment, it looks more like pony abuse than horsemanship."

Kelly made another face at him but followed his instructions well. Max moved into a slow trot.

"He won't do nothin' but poke along if'n I don' give him a good kick, Pete," Kelly insisted.

"Oh, yes he will. You just have to squeeze harder. Really squeeze, and push him along with your seat. See?"

Max cooperated by picking up his pace. Kelly was concentrating so hard she looked like she was going to burst.

"Y'all don't really mean I've gotta do this all the time, do you? Kickin's a whole lot easier."

"It may be easier, but it's not what they want to see in the show ring, that's for sure. Betsy says it's supposed to look like Max can read your mind."

"I sure hope he can't read my mind right now. He wouldn't like what he was readin', I can tell ya that!"

Keith never let Pete know he hung around for these nine o'clock lessons, but he was always within earshot. Later in the day, when Kelly and Pete had finished their chores and would take their ponies out on the trails, Keith would saddle up Ghost and go into the ring to practice everything Pete had told Kelly that morning.

Uncle Will chuckled, looking out the kitchen window. Keith was trotting figure eights in a perfect imitation of Pete's jumping position. When he settled back down into the saddle, his posture was erect, his hands were in the proper position, and his legs were under him where Pete insisted they should be.

"That boy's goin' to make rider of 'em both," Uncle Will whispered to himself.

Chapter Nine

Bubbles

"Well, would you look at that!" Kelly crowed. Keith was jumping Ghost as Pete and his cousin rounded the end of the barn. "Fancy-pants ridin'!"

The Mangy Midgets, as Keith had taken to calling them, had announced that they were going all the way out to Dawson's Mill to hunt for old bullets today. Dawson's Mill was a Civil War battlefield, and you could still find all sorts of treasures if you looked really hard.

The sky had clouded up, however, so Pete and Kelly decided instead to go over to the Simpsons' house to see Kate and Deena, who were friends of Kelly's. The Simpsons had a whole farm full of animals—goats, sheep, chickens; the works, as Pete liked to put it—so he didn't mind going along, even if he was going to be the only boy. If it got too boring, he could just go off and visit the cows or something.

But Kate and Deena weren't home, so after wolfing down the milk and cookies Mrs. Simpson offered them, Pete and Kelly headed back home. Big drops of rain were just beginning to fall as they cantered along the path that ran between the two lower pastures and back to the barn.

Pete realized he hadn't actually seen Keith on a horse in weeks. The change was instantly obvious. Keith's rangy home-trained style had given way to Pete's "proper" methods.

"He's ridin' Betsy-style!" Kelly exclaimed.

"So?" Keith glowered back at her. "What's it to you?"

"Hey, it looks great!" Pete quickly interjected. "You and Ghost look terrific. Really!"

"Well, I gotta admit, Ghost sure is jumpin' better'n ever. That's all *I* know," Keith admitted begrudgingly.

"That's all that matters," Pete pointed out. "You know—riding the way you do now you could enter an equitation class. And you'd win!"

Keith pulled Ghost to a halt. "Ya mean that?"

"Yep."

Two days later, Uncle Will announced over breakfast that at noontime he was heading over to the Milfords' place to look at a jumper for Keith and asked if anyone wanted to come. They all did, and ten minutes before noon three excited kids packed themselves into the van.

"Bubbles is what we call her. She's big, but she's jes' so light and perky, and there's somethin' 'bout the way she jes' floats over 'em fences. Named herself, she did," Jeb Milford told Keith.

Uncle Will ran a knowledgeable hand down the gray mare's legs, under her belly, across her flank. He opened her mouth, checking her teeth, then picked up her feet and inspected each hoof. Jeb led her off a bit and then trotted her up and back in front of everyone.

"Y'all can see fer yourselves, she's sound as a dollar. Never had an off day, this 'un. She's gonna make someone a fine show horse, she is. Ben," Jeb called to his stable hand, "throw a saddle 'n bridle on her and put her through her paces for the folks."

It was just like Jeb had said. The fine-boned Thorough-bred really did seem to float. Trotting, she covered ground without seeming to touch it. Her canter was smooth and elegant, and her jump looked completely effortless. Jeb kept raising the fences, and Bubbles kept jumping them.

"Want to try her?" Jeb asked Keith. Keith grinned as Jeb gave him a leg up.

He was still grinning fifteen minutes later as he slowed the tired mare back to a walk. Jeb came up to them and gave Bubbles's sweaty neck a pat.

"She could be fitter, that's the truth, but the boy's been on the road showin' the young horses, and I jes' don't have enough hands 'bout the place anymore to keep all the horses workin' out like they should. You could have her ready to show with a few weeks o' work, though." Jeb stepped back and took a long look at Keith and Bubbles. "Your boy sure does look good on her. Nice picture."

Uncle Will nodded in agreement. "You'll let us take her on trial?" The two gentlemen farmers discussed a few details, stood admiring the horse a moment longer, and then shook on the deal.

Chapter Ten

Mounting,
the Hard Way

"So Ghost is yours now, Pete. And if y'all get along good, you be plannin' on takin' him up north with you like last year, okay, boy?"

"You mean it, Uncle Will? Boy is that ever okay!" Pete was tingling with anticipation. He couldn't wait to get back to Eleven Oaks to ride the big gray. It seemed like hours before the van made the last turn and the old house and big brick stable came into view.

Uncle Will brought the van to a halt under two of the farm's eleven oaks, and Pete and Kelly scrambled out. Pete started to help unload Bubbles, but Uncle Will shooed him off. "Go and throw a saddle on your new horse, lad. I know that's what you want to be doin'." He gave Pete a playful clap on the shoulder and sent him on his way.

It didn't take long for Pete to notice some very basic differences between Lazy and Ghost Story. Size, for starters. He could look Lazy straight in the eye. Ghost might not be as big as Bubbles, but he certainly was a whole lot bigger than Lazy.

Pete brought Ghost out of his stall and put him in crossties to groom him. He scratched the horse's nose and ran his hand up the gray's face. "How about if I call you Casper, Ghost? You're friendly enough." Ghost snickered his approval of his newest stable name. "And you can call me anything you want," Pete rambled on.

Pretty soon he began to laugh. "Good grief, you're no horse—you're a giraffe," Pete said, reaching to brush the horse's forelock. He was surprised at how far he had to stretch to get to Casper's ears, and he was really amazed when he went to put on the bridle. "Now this is ridiculous," he gasped, tiptoeing like a ballet dancer as he tried to reach the bridle over the top of the horse's head.

Fortunately, no one was watching as Pete attempted to mount Casper. He just couldn't reach his foot up to the stirrup. He looked both ways to be sure there were no witnesses and then lengthened the stirrup leather as far as it went. That was a start, but it still left Pete with a real scramble to get his other leg up and over the saddle.

Once on the horse, Pete had to adjust the strap on his left stirrup, moving it back up to where it should be. Casper began to dance a nervous jig, realizing that a stranger was on his back. Tossing his head with fear, the horse began to back up while Pete was still collecting up the reins. Before Pete could stop him, Casper had backed squarely into one of the planters. Terrified, he leaped forward, and Pete went flying.

Casper took off at a gallop, the empty stirrups hanging at his sides. Pete groaned and got to his feet, more shook up than hurt. He started after the horse but hadn't gotten far before he found Keith leading Casper by the reins. The horse, nostrils flared, was panting and dancing around in fear.

"Y'all okay?" Keith asked, with genuine concern. "You don't look so good."

Pete brushed himself off and tried to laugh. "Hey, no problem. Ghost just taught me a lesson is all, didn't you, boy?" He took the reins from Keith and gave the horse a pat. "Calm down, you ol' spook."

"You're the one who looks like a ghost, little cuz,"

Keith commented. "You're white as a sheet. What happened, anyway?"

"I was just trying to mount him. He's big! It was a job getting up there. A totally screwed up job."

"That's what mountin' blocks were invented for, dummy," Keith reminded Pete, who smacked himself dramatically on the forehead.

"Oh, how could I have forgotten?"

"Beats me. Well, hey, look on the bright side. There weren't any girls around to see you sprawled in the dirt. Or guys, for that matter. That's even worse."

Pete walked Casper around for a while to calm him down and then led the gray over to the mounting block and climbed up on him gracefully. As he slipped his feet into the stirrups, he grinned over at Keith, who gave him a thumbs up in return.

"That's more like it, twerp," Keith chortled.

Chapter Eleven

Bubbles vs. Terminator

After all those months of anticipation, riding Casper was nothing like Pete had expected. Riding Casper was just plain hard.

For starters, Pete was light compared to Keith. Pete was about average size for his age, but he barely weighed seventy-seven pounds. Casper wasn't impressed. Keith weighed 124, and those extra pounds seemed to make a big difference.

Pitting his seventy-seven pounds against a thousand pounds of young horseflesh was Pete's biggest challenge. It wasn't so bad when he rode in the ring, but the minute they left its confines, Casper seemed to remember he was a Thoroughbred and would take off like a racehorse.

The first time it happened, Pete had no choice but to just ride it out. He had never run into this particular problem before, so he had no tricks up his sleeve to help him handle it. That evening he told Uncle Will what had happened.

"What can I do? I couldn't stop him. He just ran and ran and ran until he ran out of gas. I couldn't stop him, I couldn't steer him, nothing. It was his trip."

"Don't despair, boy. I'll tell ya what the jockeys do

about it. They're not a whole lot heavier than you are."
Uncle Will turned his chair around and assumed a riding
position on it.

"Okay now, say your colt's got it into his head to take
you for a ride. You take up your left rein real short and plant
it on his mane, right in front of you. Then you pull your
right rein up toward yourself and you cross right over the
mane as you're doin' it. You're goin' to turn his head that
way and pull him 'round in a tight circle, that's what you're
goin' to be doin'. An' you jes' keep pullin' him 'round till
he comes to a stop."

Pete listened attentively. "Left rein planted, right rein
pulled over his mane?"

"That's it. Or the other way 'round, whichever suits
you. I've always preferred clockwise, m'self. See if'n that
don't do the job. If y'all are still feudin', I s'pose we could
try out some tougher bits, but I'd rather see you handlin'
him with jes' a pelham." Pete was anxious to give Uncle
Will's suggestion a try.

"Okay, Casper, here's your big chance to do your
worst," he whispered to the gray the next morning. "I'm
ready for you. Today, it's gonna be a fair fight."

Casper took the challenge, but Pete came out the winner. After several attempts to take off, Casper finally seemed
to accept the fact that running away was going to get him
nowhere. "Nowhere but dizzy, you dumb horse." Pete
laughed.

"Bubbles, she's a jumpin' fool, she is," Keith announced to no one in particular over dinner one evening.
No one disagreed. Keith and Bubbles were getting along
great.

"So, Pa, when can I let the rest of the world in on the
secret?" he wanted to know. "Can I take her to a show
before Pete has to go on back home? I sure could use the
pipsqueak in my cheerin' section. Lemme hear y'all cheer,
kid."

Pete let out a couple of good hollers.

"Yep. Can't let talent like that get outa the state, now

can we? I sorta had my eye on the big show over in Greensboro for Bubbles to make her debut."

"What's a day-bue?" Pete asked.

"What's a debut?" Keith looked suitably horrified. "Hey, don't they teach y'all no French up there in Yankee land? A debut? A debut is, um, well it's like a first time out— the first time on the stage, or the first time playin' in a baseball game . . . a first for any ol' thing."

"Hey, yeah, I'd like to see Bubbles's first show. I could help and everything. And yell."

"Well, Pete, y'all practice your yellin' then, and I'll see 'bout entries. If that's what you've got your heart set on, son," Uncle Will told Keith, "it's okay with me."

The Greensboro show was the biggest show Pete had ever been to. It was a five-day event, and temporary stabling had been put up under several big green-and-white tents. Over four hundred horses were entered.

"Aren't you totally terrified, Keith? Shaking in your boots? Sick to your stomach? I mean, aren't you scared to death?"

"Thanks, Pete. Believe it or not, I was doin' jes' fine till you started in on me. Like they's always sayin', with friends like y'all, who needs enemies?"

"Gee, I'm sorry," Pete started to apologize. "But, gosh, did you know there're forty-four horses in the preliminary jumper division? And that's just what's listed in the program. Who knows how many late entries they got! That's one heck of a lot of horses."

Keith made a menacing face at Pete. "Shut up or beat it, kid, you hear me?"

"Okay, okay, I won't say any more. I promise." Pete quickly set to work making himself useful.

Pete was on the rail for Keith's first class. Seventeen horses had jumped by the time Bubbles entered the ring. Of those, only three had gone over clearly. Bubbles put in a perfect trip, becoming the fourth. Pete yelled his head off. By the end of the first round of jumping, only eight were still in it.

The jump crew raised the fences and the eight jumped the course for the second time. Bubbles again put in a clean performance, with Pete whooping it up after each and every fence. This time, only one other entry went clean, a huge black horse called Terminator. The fences were raised again.

Keith and Bubbles jumped first. They made a big circle at the end of the ring, and then Keith headed Bubbles for the first fence, a white gate with three red-and-white striped rails above it. Pete gasped as he clearly heard one of Bubbles's hooves graze the top rail as she went over. His heart sank as he watched the rail roll slowly, lazily off the standards. He hardly breathed as Bubbles continued on around the course. The horse went over every other fence perfectly.

"That's four faults on Bubbles, Number 232," boomed the announcer. "Next to jump is Terminator, Number 344."

Terminator entered the ring. Pete watched stony-faced as the big horse cleared the first four jumps. On the fifth jump, a large spread fence coming off a sharp turn, his rider misjudged his takeoff. The horse brought down the entire jump, costing Terminator four faults.

It's not fair, Pete thought to himself. Keith only took down one measly rail. This guy totaled that fence. He should get more like a *hundred* and four faults.

Terminator continued on, over the wall and the coop, and down to the three-fence combination that ended the course. Pete suddenly saw that Terminator's timing was off as the horse approached the first of the three fences.

"He's doomed," Pete whispered to himself as the horse took off too early on the first jump. He should have taken two strides before the second jump, but ended up putting in three choppy ones instead and brought the top rail down as he somehow scrambled over it. He never even tried to jump the third fence but plowed into it anyway, scattering rails in all directions.

Keith had just won his first class with Bubbles.

Chapter Twelve

Casper Meets
the Iron Lady

I t was one of those amazing shows—Bubbles could do no
wrong. Class after class, day after day, he just kept putting in one excellent performance after another. After
the last of the preliminary jumper classes was over, points
were tallied. Keith and Bubbles were called into the ring to
accept the blue, red, and yellow championship ribbon, a large
silver bowl, and the applause of an audience that recognized
a great young horse when it saw one.

The show over, an elated and weary Eleven Oaks crew
packed up and headed home. Keith was sitting by the window and fell asleep before they had even left the show
grounds. Pete was sitting next to Uncle Will. They kept their
voices low so they wouldn't disturb the snoring champion.

"That championship is part yours. Ya know that, don't
you?" Uncle Will asked his nephew. Pete shrugged. "Hey, I
didn't do all that much. Maybe I helped with the grooming
and stuff, but I was glad to. It was fun."

"You did more'n you know, boy. Why, Keith wouldn't
be half the rider he is if'n it weren't for your trainin'."

41

"What do you mean? I taught Kelly the stuff I know, but Keith wouldn't have anything to do with it."

"Maybe not in front of you, but I happen to know he worked jes' as hard at it as Kelly. Harder. He sure never learned that kinda ridin' from me."

Pete basked in his uncle's praise. The two fell silent as Uncle Will drove the van on through the night. Now that the Greensboro show was over, Pete started thinking about his trip home. Would Betsy be impressed with his new horse and how he rode him?

They pulled out of the driveway at Eleven Oaks well before dawn. Pete had made the trip home from Royalton many times, but it had never seemed as endless as it did today. The van crawled up through Virginia, past Washington, D.C., and across little bits of Maryland and Delaware. Pete and his uncle both let out big sighs as the "Welcome to New Jersey" sign finally flashed by.

Even the Jersey leg of the trip, as Uncle Will always called it, seemed to take forever. It was well after sunset when the van rolled up to the stable door at Dutch Mill. Pete was disappointed that none of the kids would be there to greet him. At least the light in Betsy's office was still burning.

"Well, now, that's what I call a horse!" Betsy exclaimed, as Pete led Casper down the ramp.

"Betsy, I'd like you to meet Ghost Story, alias Ghost, alias Casper. Casper, this is Betsy—alias the Iron Lady."

Betsy couldn't find enough nice things to say about the gray, and Uncle Will enjoyed her enthusiasm every bit as much as Pete did. She was just as impressed the next morning as she watched Pete put him through his paces for her.

"The way he moves is wonderful! He's beautifully built, and he's really supple. It looks like you've really been working hard with him. Has he been shown at all?"

"Keith showed him last year in junior hunters," Pete shouted over his shoulder as he trotted a tight circle. "Did pretty well. Won a bunch of ribbons and took one reserve. But he said Casper was inconsistent. I think he's going pretty good now." Pete brought Casper into the center of the ring where Betsy was perched on the top rail of a fence. He gave the horse an appreciative pat.

"*Pretty* good? I'd say very good! I can tell he's a handful for you, but you seem to have things well under control. What's he like on the trails?"

"Like Secretariat," Pete joked, referring to the Triple Crown winner. "Only Uncle Will could teach me how to hold him. I call it a jockey-stop. You run him in circles till he gives up. It works."

"Pete, I am so pleased for you. You've really got a show horse now!" Pete's face glowed with happiness. "Let's do a little polishing, and then let's find you some shows."

Pete's friends were just as enthusiastic about Casper. Alexis decided he was "awesome." "Great" and "gorgeous" were Meg and Morgan's words for him. Mel offered to braid him for free for his first show. She called it her "get acquainted offer" and hoped Pete would like her braiding well enough to ask her to do it for him all the time.

Chapter Thirteen

Can You Tell Me What My Number Is?

"I didn't know Uncle Will was going to let you bring home such a *big* horse, Petey," said Mrs. Draper nervously when she first saw Casper.

"He's not that big, Mom. Anyway, you don't have to worry. This one's full grown, too. At least he won't be getting any bigger."

Casper tried to make friends with Mrs. Draper by sniffing at her neck just as she turned to answer Pete. She stifled a scream and rushed out of Casper's stall faster than Pete had ever seen her move.

"Oh, Petey! I'll—I'll never understand what you see in horses," she stammered as she tried to collect what was left of her dignity. "I'm sorry, Casper. I'll come and watch you at horse shows, but I don't think I'll be paying you any more visits in your stall!"

True to her word, two weeks later Pete's mother was sitting in the grandstand waiting for Pete's first class to begin. It was a local schooling show at Saddle Park. Mrs. Draper was just about the only mother in the stands, probably because of the light but steady rain that was falling. Over the loudspeaker, the announcer had assured everyone that unless things got worse the show would be proceeding right on schedule. The first class would be the Fourteen-and-Under Novice Over Fences. Pete's mother sat under her golf umbrella and tried to remember what that meant.

All the riders had put clear plastic rain jackets and hat covers over their show clothes. Betsy held Casper as Pete tried to tie his number around his waist. His hands were shaking.

"Hey, relax, kiddo," Betsy told him. "Weren't you the guy who was complaining that this wasn't a big enough show to bother with? Weren't you the one who wanted your first show with Casper to be at Madison Square Garden?"

Pete looked at her sheepishly and tried to calm down. "Hey, just think of it as a warm-up class, Pete. Do what I used to do—pretend this one doesn't count!" Pete grinned and Betsy continued.

"The fences are small, no worries there. The footing is getting a little heavy with the rain, but really, that's probably for the best. Casper's a little excited. Working his way through the stuff will slow him down a bit."

"I'll be okay if I just don't go off course," Pete joked. The course was simple—twice around, over four, two-foot three-inch fences.

"Just remember, this may be a novice class, and I know you've never won three blues, but you've got more experience in the ring than most of these kids. It's just that you spent so much time showing poor old invisible Lazy. They're going to see you this time!"

Pete was jumping third. He watched the first two riders go, took a deep breath, and then headed into the ring. He moved Casper into a trot and then a canter, making a big circle. The horse swished his tail nervously and then settled down to business as he headed for the first fence.

Pete kept the refrain "This one doesn't count, this is just a warm-up" running through his mind, and suddenly he felt himself relax. A smile actually came to his face. Just as suddenly, a new thought hit him. This was going to be fun!

Pete's round was excellent—proof that positive thinking

helps. It seemed like only moments had passed when he found himself pulling the gray back to a trot and heading for the Out gate. Even before he saw Betsy's grin, he knew he'd ridden very well. He was immediately surrounded by several other Dutch Mill kids, all congratulating him noisily. He felt terrific.

The rain had tapered off and it almost looked like the sun was going to break through the clouds. Pete walked Casper for what felt like hours, waiting for the rest of the riders to jump. There were twenty-four in all.

"Would the following riders please return to the ring . . . ," the loudspeaker finally announced. Pete froze. What was his number?

"Numbers 118, 56, 39, 88, 17 and 106. I repeat, 118, 56, 39, 88, 17 and 106, to the ring, please."

Pete grabbed the rider next to him, turned his back to him, and asked him to tell him what his number was.

"Boy are you out of it! It's thirty-nine."

"Third!" Pete grinned and trotted quickly into the ring. The six horses lined up and the ringmaster awarded them their ribbons. Pete thought Casper looked great with the yellow ribbon pinned to his bridle.

Chapter Fourteen

Jasper, Freddy, Lucius, and Hump

"Do you know who that is?" Jonathan whispered to Pete and Julia as one of the judges walked by them.

"No," Julia answered for both of them.

"I didn't think so. That's just Greg Mersio, is all," Jonathan informed them.

Jonathan had been showing at all the big shows for years and was considered Dutch Mill's resident expert on who was who on the show circuit.

Julia finally made his day by asking, "Okay—who is Greg Mersio?"

"Only one of the top trainers in the country. What he's doing judging at a rinky-dink, leaky-roof little show like this, I don't know. He's the only reason I decided to come, myself."

As soon as Jonathan left, Julia and Pete looked at each other and cracked up.

"That guy is such a stuffed shirt," Julia giggled. " 'He's the only reason I decided to come.' Did you hear that? I'll tell you the only reason I came. This is a small enough show that I have half a chance of winning some ribbons. I never even looked at who was judging."

"Me either. Besides, the name wouldn't have meant anything to me even if I had. I came because Betsy said I should," Pete said with a laugh. But he found himself looking at the famous judge with interest and just a little nervousness.

Pete's second class of the day was the Maiden on the Flat, a non-jumping class for riders who had never won a blue ribbon. He felt like he had a good chance in this class, considering the amount of time he had spent over the last few months working Casper. He was as ready as he'd ever be.

What he wasn't ready for was the combination of seeing Greg Mersio standing in the middle of the ring and Jasper MacMillan sitting in the stands. What was a big-shot trainer like Greg Mersio doing judging a beginners' class like the Maiden? And why did Jasper have to be there. Pete felt close to panic.

The second time he came around by the grandstand, he understood Jasper's presence. He was sitting with Tracy Field's brother Freddy. Freddy was there to watch Tracy ride. Freddy and Jasper were both in Pete's sixth grade class in school, and they hung out together a lot.

"Oh, no," Pete gasped under his breath. True to form, Freddy and Jasper's shadows were there, too—good old Lucius and Hump. Hump had to be the unluckiest kid ever named. There weren't many other possible nicknames for Humphrey, and his middle name was Rutledge, one of the best kept secrets of the twentieth century. The only thing he could thank his parents for was not producing any sisters or brothers to spread the word around.

"Hey, look at Petey," came the unmistakably low-pitched voice of Jasper MacMillan. "Look at Petey in a ring full of girls!"

Pete felt his face go beet red as he suddenly looked around him and realized that he was, in fact, the only boy in the ring. The voice on the loudspeaker announced, "Trot, please. All trot."

Pete tried to stay as far away from the railing as he could the next time around, but he could still hear loud and clear when Hump started hooting, "What's a boy doing in the *Maiden* class?"

Pete tried to force his concentration back on his riding, but the third time he came by the stands, all four boys were rehearsed and waiting for him. "Petey's not going to be a maiden for long, not in that ring full of girls," they sang out in unison. "Canter, please. All canter," came the announcer's call.

Pete did something he had never done to Casper before. He was so upset that he dug his right heel into the horse's ribs, almost viciously. All he could think of was getting away from the heckling voices.

Casper suddenly took the bit in his teeth, bolted, and ran. Pete realized too late what he'd done and hauled back on the reins, but Casper was beyond noticing. Pete groaned as it hit him that the ring was way too crowded for him to use his jockey-stop. If he turned in a circle, he'd run into a million girls.

All he could do was try to avoid running anyone over. He watched for openings as Casper galloped uncontrollably through the crowd of cantering horses and ponies. Pete was doing okay until he and Casper blazed by the grandstand one more time.

"Petey!" his mother shrieked in horror, jumping to her feet as she realized that her son's horse was out of control. Casper saw her out of the corner of his eye, shied, bucked, and came lurching to a halt. Pete went flying.

At that moment, Pete decided that there was definitely something worse than being the only boy in the ring.

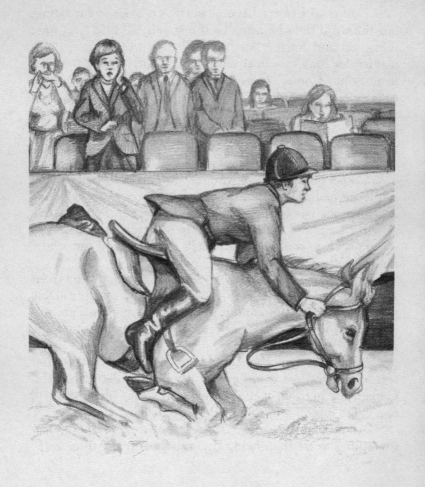

Chapter Fifteen

"You've Got Talent, Kid"

Casper sent a nervous shudder through the crowd as he took off through the ring full of riders—his reins trailing on the ground.

Only luck kept the panicked horse from stepping on them, or worse yet, catching a foot in them in his headlong gallop. As it was, he finally came to a halt and allowed one of the jump crew to approach him and lead him over to the Out gate. Pete fought back tears of humiliation as he accepted the reins and led his horse from the ring in disgrace.

Silently, Pete took Casper back to the Dutch Mill van and untacked him. Not speaking to anyone, he put a halter on the horse, sponged him down, and walked him until he was cool. He put Casper back in the van, struggled out of his jacket and tie and unbuttoned the collar of his shirt.

The van was pulled up alongside a rock wall. Pete went around to the wall. He climbed over it, sat down, and leaned back against it. The rocks poked into his back, but somehow it just felt right. His head sagged and he covered his eyes. He tried to make his mind go blank, but all it would do was show him instant replays of the Maiden class.

51

He didn't know how long he'd been sitting there when he heard a voice ask someone by the van, "Has anyone seen Pete Draper? He rides with you all, doesn't he?"

Pete heard Celia answer. "Yeah, he does. At least, I think he still does. He may have given up riding altogether by now."

The voice asked, "Do you know where I could find him?" It was a man's voice.

Pete cringed as he heard Tracy tell him that she'd seen him back behind the van, on the other side of the wall. So much for privacy. He was still sitting with his head in his hands when a pair of tan loafers and brown corduroys came into view in front of him.

Pete looked up reluctantly and recognized the weathered face before him. He scrambled to his feet in confusion.

"Hi, I'm Greg Mersio," the judge said with a friendly smile. He put out his hand. Pete shook it dumbly.

"And you're Pete Draper, right?" Pete nodded. Greg could tell he was going to have to conduct a one-man conversation until Pete recovered his composure.

"Pretty embarrassing, what happened back there," Greg went on. "I really felt for you, kid." Pete blinked.

"I could hear those guys heckling you. Nothing worse. I know, it's happened to me a few times, too. I don't think I'll ever forget what it felt like. Seeing you go through it today really brought it back."

Pete felt like he'd never speak again, but he somehow managed to choke out, "You?"

"Yep. Once when I was nine, and then, let's see . . . when I was fourteen, and then again the next year, I think. The one when I was fourteen was the worst, the absolute worst.

"You know what happened? This girl I was crazy about was sitting in the bleachers. I was riding in a hunter hack class, on the flat, just like you. I was riding this chestnut mare, a wonderful horse named Red. Great horse.

"Anyway, here I was, warming up, feeling good—you know, that feeling you get when you can actually imagine yourself winning the class? And I noticed DeeDee in the stands. I started getting all self-conscious and nervous. And then I noticed that she wasn't by herself, that this guy I knew was sitting by her. He had his arm around her, as a matter of fact.

"That was bad enough, but then I clearly heard him saying to her, loud enough for the whole county to hear, 'You don't have to worry about Greg. Look at him. He's got a whole ringful of girls to himself.' People heard him, too, because the next thing I knew a bunch of little kids had started saying it." Greg paused and then sat down next to Pete.

"You're probably wondering what happened then . . . oh, nothing much. I went scarlet; Red went purple and took off with me. Spooked a bunch of other horses and the whole ring went crazy. Three people ended up on the ground. I was so mortified that I found myself wishing I was one of them. *They* got to leave the ring. Me, I had to finish the class. Needless to say, I didn't get anything but a whole lot more embarrassed. I almost gave up riding that day."

Pete started to giggle in spite of himself. "That bad?"

"That bad."

"But you didn't quit."

"Nope."

"I might."

"Aw, come on, Pete. It's just one of the knocks of being a guy who rides. I've never heard what the statistics are, but I'll bet you there must be ten thousand girls for every guy who rides. Hell, maybe not quite ten thousand, but there sure are a whole slew of 'em.

"But you want to know something interesting? Out of all those girls, probably ninety-seven percent of them'll quit before they finish high school. Or college, anyway. But— here's the interesting part—most of the boys who're good riders at your age stay with it and go on to become pros."

Pete looked up at Greg, surprised.

"Yup, professionals. You know what else? I think *you're* a good rider. I get a kick out of spotting good new riders, especially if they're boys. And you're definitely good!

"Don't get me wrong. I'd never give you a ribbon just

because you're a boy. But I'll tell you, you're one kid I plan to keep an eye on. You've got talent, kid. And you know something else? Someday, I bet you'll even learn how to speak!" he teased.

Greg got to his feet and dusted himself off. "I've got to be getting back to the show. See you later?"

Pete looked up and grinned. "Yeah. I'll be there."